Nature makes great scents.

Thanks!

Kirby & Cindy

Earl

Pearl

HAPPY TAILS
The Call of Nature

**Photographs and story
by Cindy and Kirby Pringle**

Dedicated to Barney and Buster, the best dogs ever.

Also by the authors:
"Happy Tails: Earl and Pearl on the Farm"

Visit Earl and Pearl at:
www.dogtownartworks.com

Copyright © 2008 Cindy and Kirby Pringle
Published by Dogtown Artworks, USA

First Printing: May 2008
ISBN 978-0-9777126-1-8
10 9 8 7 6 5 4 3 2 1
LCCN 2008900444

Printed in Canada by Friesens

Mixed Sources
Product group from well-managed forests and other controlled sources
www.fsc.org Cert no. SW-COC-1271
© 1996 Forest Stewardship Council

FSC

P earl Barker's pink nails click rapidly across the keyboard.

"Dear Earlene, please write me as SOON as you get this! You MUST tell me about the cat show that you will be judging! LOL (Lots of Licks!), Pearl."

Pearl waits a few minutes and when Earlene, her best friend and her husband Earl's twin sister, doesn't respond, she picks up the BoneFone and tries to call, but gets only the voicemail.

"Oh dear! She must have her phone turned off. Maybe I should

try to text her! Or should I send an instant message? It's been over an hour since I last heard from her. Maybe her Internet service is down again! Maybe I should send myself an e-mail to make sure my Internet service is working!"

Pearl's whiskers quiver, her nose glistens — she's anxious. Very anxious. She misses Earlene terribly and has for months. Earlene headed west for her dream job — to be a professional cat show judge. Earlene loves everything about cats, from the way they purr to their fluffy, soft fur.

To keep in touch with Earlene, Pearl bought her first computer and cell phone, a pretty pink one shaped like a bone. They send messages constantly — so many that Pearl isn't getting anything else done around the house or on the farm. Pearl even has her own blog and social networking site, so she has lots of friends on the Web to stay in touch with. She can barely keep track of them all.

Pearl also connected all the farm buildings — even the outhouse — to a wireless network so that she can get online anywhere she wants.

Earlene loves to shop online, especially for her cats. She buys rubber mice, pretty collars, soft little beds and such. She finds a Web site that offers dainty party dresses, just for cats. Earlene wonders what her orange tabby, Hazelnut, would look like in a blue party dress. "Oh, how silly. Who could imagine a cat in a dress? ME-OW!" she says to Hazelnut and giggles. Earlene sometimes likes to end sentences with a long and high-pitched, "ME-OW!"

When she checks her e-mail, she finds six frantic messages from Pearl — all with big black exclamation marks. She worries about Pearl, who sends an endless stream of e-mails. Earlene misses the days when Pearl mailed handwritten notes and cards. Pearl was always so clever with her notes. But now everything is an abbreviation: LOL, AWDY, OB, RL. Earlene doesn't know what most of them mean. She wishes she could have a long talk with Pearl — in person.

On occasion, Pearl puts away the laptop and grabs a broom to entertain the chickens. She turns on her iPaw, strikes a chord on her straw guitar and does karaoke for the hens. The chickens cluck and dance with her.

"Happy hens lay bigger eggs," Pearl says to herself. "And they love to hear me sing. Modern technology is so sweet! I can do karaoke, check my e-mail in the hen house, find hidden eggs with my GPS unit — hey, maybe I should put a webcam in here! Then I can put on my site, 'Click here for clucks!'

"Dance, chickies, dance!"

E arl is not much of a cook. Pearl always seems so busy, checking and sending e-mail, talking with Earlene on the BoneFone. She doesn't have much time for Earl. And so he makes lots of toast for his meals. But he's getting tired of all that bread. When he burns his toast to a crisp, it's just too much.

"Pearl!" he howls. "This is it! My toast is burned. You've become a tech-hound and the farm is falling apart. We're going on a vacation! Right now! C'mon, Pearl, pack your things. Our neighbor can watch the farm for a while. We're going to visit Earlene and along the way we're going hiking, camping, boating — and no toast! I'm going toast-free, but can you get by without your cell phone and laptop? I have my doubts."

P earl quickly packs. But she's in such a hurry — she just has to call Earlene and tell her the news — that she doesn't notice a few things are missing from her suitcase. Earl hides the phone charger, the power cord to the laptop and all the extra batteries under the living room sofa. He calls his plan, "Pearl Unplugged."

Earl pulls their car, LuLu, out of the shed and waits for Pearl to finish her call. She can't seem to put the phone away — a tornado couldn't blow it out of her paw.

"Pearl, please get in the car! You can talk on the road!" Earl says. "Come, girl, c'mon!"

"Don't get your fur up. I'm trying to talk to Earlene. And can you move LuLu? I think she's causing some kind of interference," Pearl replies.

On the way to Earlene's house, Earl spots a cute little gas station, Flip's 66. A station attendant pumps the gas and washes the windshield. Earl can't believe it.

"Check your tires? Check your oil? Brush your fur?" the attendant asks.

Pearl studies the map while Earl pays for the gas. The GPS unit in LuLu is on the fritz.

"Wow! What great service!" Earl tells Pearl. "I didn't even know places like this existed anymore. Don't you just love getting off the beaten path and exploring?"

"Oh yes! I love to get out my laptop and look up roadside attractions, like BoneHenge," Pearl says. "It's quite the tasty tourist attraction — an ancient and mysterious sundial made of giant, stone biscuits. Mmmm, biscuits. Let's get some chow!"

7

As they cruise down the two-lane highway, going through all the cute little towns with their quaint businesses, Pearl spots a sign and squeals, "PULL OVER!" Earl hits the brakes, looks over and sees "The Gravy Boat Cafe" in big white letters on a red awning that stretches across the front of the restaurant. Pearl adores gravy. A note on the door says water is served in a glass or a bowl — just the kind of place for Earl and Pearl.

Annie, their waitress, asks Pearl for her order.

"I'd like the spaghetti and gravy special with taters and gravy, beets and gravy, and applesauce and gravy. For dessert, I'll have the brownie and gravy," Pearl says and licks her chops. "And could I please get extra gravy on the side?"

While Earl heads to the bank, Pearl slips out of the car, opens the trunk and gets out her laptop. Fortunately, the laundry across the street has wi-fi — she hopes. The sign painter misspelled the name. She needs to write her blog and send out a bulletin to her online friends that she might not be able to respond to their messages as quickly as she usually does — which is instantly. She also wants to check her e-mail and write Earlene. These things are extremely important.

"How does Earl expect me to stay in touch with my friends? Howl in the night? How old school," she thinks to herself as she taps on the keyboard.

E arl and Pearl find a nice, isolated camping spot to spend the night. He decides to start the fire by rubbing two sticks together — just like he did in his Pup Scout days.

Pearl pulls her laptop from the bag and shows Earl her new "flaming log" screensaver.

"See, Earl, computers are good for all sorts of things! I can start a fire much faster than you. Ha!" Pearl says.

"Well, I'll keep that in mind tonight when I'm roasting marshmallows over the fire. What will you be having? Virtual s'mores?" Earl replies.

Suddenly, the laptop screen goes blank. The battery is dead and Pearl wrinkles her muzzle.

"The fun just went out of the vacation," she says.

The next morning, Earl tells Pearl that he left the power cord and extra battery for her computer at home. She's not a happy camper.

"Untether yourself, Pearl! Free yourself from your digital lifeline! We're going to have so much fun, you'll forget all about the laptop. Let's have a cup of coffee on the pier before we take our shower," he says.

Earl and Pearl are camping at Lake Wetwater — it has a twin, Lake Drywater, which isn't nearly as popular.

"Look how beautiful this is, Pearl. The water, the trees, the warm sunshine. Let's drive to the ocean! It's not far," he says.

"Whatever," a grumpy Pearl replies. "That way you could work on your tan — I need sunglasses when I look at you!"

E arl and Pearl warm their fur on the sandy beach.

"Pearl, please put your cell phone down and listen to the ocean. Grab a seashell and put it up to your ear — you can hear the ocean waves!" Earl says excitedly.

"Earl, I am listening to the ocean. I'm connected to Dial-an-Ocean, which only charges 10 cents a minute to listen to the sea. And for only a nickel more they will throw in the sound of seagulls. It's a really good deal," she says.

"It's not that good of a deal," Earl says. "We're at the ocean! Put your BoneFone away! Take a look at the sea, the sand, the sun! Enjoy nature and the world around you. Take a deep breath of that fresh ocean air. Think how lucky we are to be alive!"

"And to have cell phones!" Pearl says. Suddenly the BoneFone goes dead. She's horrified. "Oh, no! The battery just died."

"Good thing my shell doesn't need a battery!" Earl says.

Only one thing can calm Pearl's frazzled nerves: ice cream.

They find a cute dairy bar, the Twistee Treat, in Tick Creek, not far from the beach. Pearl's mood brightens as they drive up. As soon as she sees the giant cone, a thin line of drool slides down the corner of her jowl.

"A vanilla cone! Make mine a large one!" she says.

Earl hustles to the window because Pearl is dripping slobber on LuLu's floorboard. Now he's really hungry, too, and can't wait for his cone. Before he gets back to the car, Earl takes two big licks of his cone and then sticks it in his mouth. It tastes sooooo good. The cold chills his tongue.

"Earl, give me my cone before you eat it too!" Pearl says. "You should take your time and enjoy your cone instead of wolfing it down in one bite. Besides, I think you've got more ice cream on your nose than you do in your mouth!"

The end of the cone suddenly disappears as Earl swallows the rest of the ice cream in one big, lip-smacking gulp. Then he turns around and points to the Twistee Treat.

"Imagine if we had that cone in our house! We could have ice cream every day for a year!" Earl says.

"Imagine if that was a big cell phone, I'd call it a ConeFone and could make calls for a year without the battery running down!" Pearl says with a laugh. "How could you leave the power cord to my computer at home, anyway? And the cell phone charger, too! It's almost like you did it on purpose."

"Maybe," Earl says and breaks into a wide grin. "Admit it, though, you're still having fun!"

"I'd have more fun," she says, "if you buy me another cone."

Earl, with a bit of begging, convinces Pearl that going for a long hike will make her feel better and help her withdrawal symptoms.

With the battery dead on the BoneFone, Pearl can't make calls. The laptop is useless, too. And they are in the middle of nowhere, far from the nearest phone store or computer shop.

"I'm in a digital wasteland," she moans. "I couldn't make a call if I wanted to — I can't see a cell phone tower anywhere."

"Pearl, don't be such a stick in the mud," Earl says. "A stick in the mouth is much better!"

The hikes, the camping, the picnics, gliding down a green river in a canoe — all are slowly having an effect on Pearl. She won't admit it to Earl, but she's having a blast being outdoors. There's so much to see, so much to do, so much to sniff! Pearl even insists on going birdwatching, one of her favorite hobbies that had gone by the wayside after she started spending so much time on the laptop and BoneFone. In the woods, Pearl spots a cuckoo through the binoculars. Then it suddenly flies out of sight.

"Earl! Where did that cuckoo go? Do you see it?" she asks.

"I sure do," Earl says. "In fact, I see two of them!"

Earlene visits the beauty parlor to get her hair done for Earl and Pearl's visit. She hasn't seen her relatives for more than a year, so she's a little nervous. Earlene decides to get a shampoo and set.

"Earl and Pearl haven't seen me with my curly hair yet," she thinks to herself. "I hope they don't mistake me for a poodle!" She studies Bone Appétit magazine, trying to decide what to fix for her family.

"Yum!" she says, her mouth watering. "This shepherd's pie looks so delicious. I could take a bite right out of the page! I'm such a bad girl! ME-OW!"

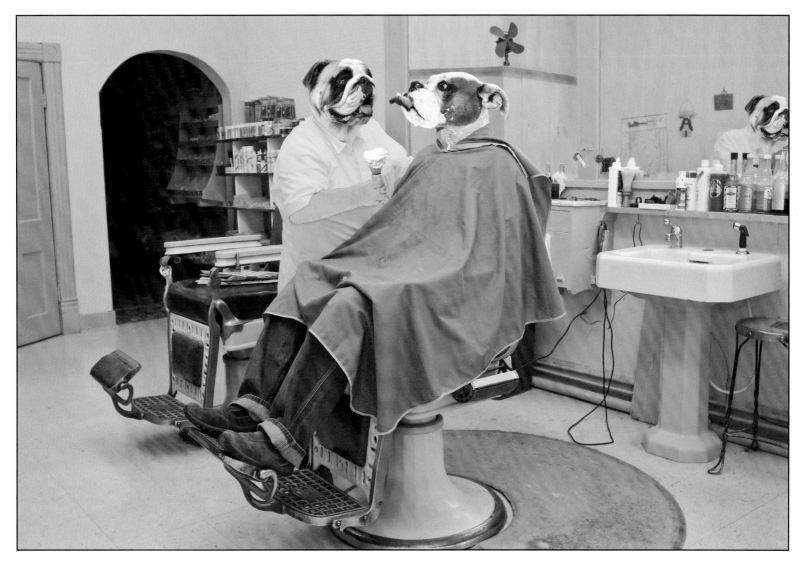

Earl, too, decides to get his whiskers trimmed to look nice and neat for his twin sister. He stops at Tiny's Barbershop and tells Tiny, "Give me the works, please!"

As Tiny brushes the white foam around Earl's muzzle, he gets a dab on Earl's upper lip.

"Hey, that tastes pretty good!" Earl says after he takes a lick. "What brand is that shaving cream?"

"Whipped cream! My wife made it up this morning. I ran out of the regular shaving cream," Tiny says. "Lick as much as you want — although not too much. I have to save some for my pumpkin pie tonight."

Walnut, another of Earlene's cats, takes a catnap and doesn't even open his eyes when a car stops in front of the house.

"I'm so glad you made it!" Earlene says as Earl and Pearl step onto the sidewalk. "I hadn't heard from you for several days and couldn't reach Pearl on her cell phone. Oh well, doesn't matter. You got here safe and sound. Now sit down and have a glass of pink lemonade before you come inside. Just don't sit on my cat. He's sensitive about that!"

"I would have called or sent an e-mail, but Earl left the chargers for the laptop and BoneFone at home," Pearl says.

"You poor thing. Perhaps it's for the best, though. Pearl, you did go overboard on the whole tech thing. Just do like me and turn those digital lemons into lemonade!"

The next day, Earlene takes her guests to the park for a cookout. Earl volunteers to grill the veggie burgers, although Earlene makes him wear a fur-net.

"Food safety, Earl. The last time we cooked out, everyone had all these white hairs in their food. And we know who has male-pattern shedding in this family!" Earlene says. "We know it's not me. My hair is naturally curly — ME-OW! — and I never shed."

"You won't find one hair on your burger, Earlene. I licked it clean!" Earl says and sticks out his tongue. "Tasty. And properly cooked!"

E arl, Pearl and Earlene go for long walks during the day and play board games at night. They sit around the kitchen table and talk, munching on cookies as steam whirls from the spout of a cat-shaped teakettle on the stove.

One afternoon, Pearl suggests that the three of them go to the park and play.

"Let's go swing, just like we used to do when we were all pups," Pearl says. "You're never too old for fur-raising fun!"

Earl straps on a cowboy hat, just like he did when he was little.

"Yee-hah!" Earl says. "This is more fun than sticking your head out the car window!"

E arlene drives them to one of her favorite spots, a tallgrass prairie that's full of flowers and wildlife. Pearl takes a big whiff from a vivid patch of yellow wildflowers and gets a drop of nectar on her nose.

Suddenly, flitting aimlessly along, a monarch butterfly lands on the tip of her nose and starts sipping the nectar.

"Oh goodness, that tickles," Pearl says.

Earl watches the butterfly as it slowly fans its wings and Pearl looks on in amazement.

"See, Pearl," he says, "I always said you were made of sugar and spice and everything nice!"

As a going-away present, Earlene buys a matching pair of sunflower hats for Earl and Pearl.

"They go perfectly with your little yellow car. Now you can have a flower in your bud vase and flowers on top of your heads at the same time," Earlene says.

Earl and Pearl put on the hats and wave goodbye to Earlene.

"Thank you so much for a wonderful time," Pearl says. "And I promise to write often — on the new stationery you got me. I might still e-mail you, just not 20 times a day."

"You scared me for a second. I thought you were going to say, 'I'll be stationary in front of the computer all day!'" Earlene says. "Always remember, Pearl, a flower needs sunshine to bloom. ME-OW!"

After Earl and Pearl leave, Earlene drives to the annual Canine Cat Fanciers Federation National Championship, where she's the head judge. She tests the cats' agility, attentiveness and playfulness — also their scent. This one, Ferdinand, smells really good, like grilled salmon.

Some of the other cats in the show don't have a nice odor. She sniffs one and thinks, "Talcum powder." Another reminds her of a banana. "What a fruity cat," she says. One cat even smells like a rotten egg — "Yuck, you're not going home with a ribbon."

Instead, she awards Ferdinand first place for "Best Smelling Cat."

"I could take you home and sniff you all night," she says and gives Ferdinand a wet lick across his face. "You taste pretty good, too. But we don't have an award for that."

On the way home, Pearl can't wait to get outside and play at every opportunity. She's carefree and phone-free. No calls. No text messages. No e-mail. No updating her blog every hour. And she doesn't miss any of it. Pearl asks Earl to pull over alongside a wide grassy field so they can run and stretch their legs.

"Fetch this Earl!" Pearl says as she tosses the pink disc. "Jump! Good boy! I haven't seen you jump so high since the time I dropped that ice cube down the back of your overalls."

The next afternoon, they discover the Lucky Goat Rescue Ranch, where the owner, Duke Darling, rescues unwanted and abused goats from all over the country.

One of the goats likes to climb on top of Duke's antique car.

"The only way I can get that goat off my car is to play a polka on the accordion," Duke says.

"Really?" Earl asks. "I used to play the accordion. Do you mind if I give it a try?"

Duke hands Earl the accordion. He straps it on, walks up to the car and plays "The Billy Goat Polka." And sure enough, the goat goes to the edge of the car, shuffles his hooves a bit and jumps right off.

D uke built his goats a wonderful brick tower. They love to climb the spiral steps and rest inside on the hay-covered floor. The goat tower, awash in gold light from the setting sun, captivates Pearl. She quickly grabs the new paint set she bought at a town only a few miles back. The goats make a high-pitched "baaaah," sounding almost like sheep, as she paints the tower. A wave of pure joy rushes through her.

"The goats really enjoy climbing that tower. Maybe I'll even join them after I finish my painting," Pearl says to herself. "I just have to write a note to Earlene and tell her about the goat ranch. She'll probably want a tower for her cats — carpeted, of course!"

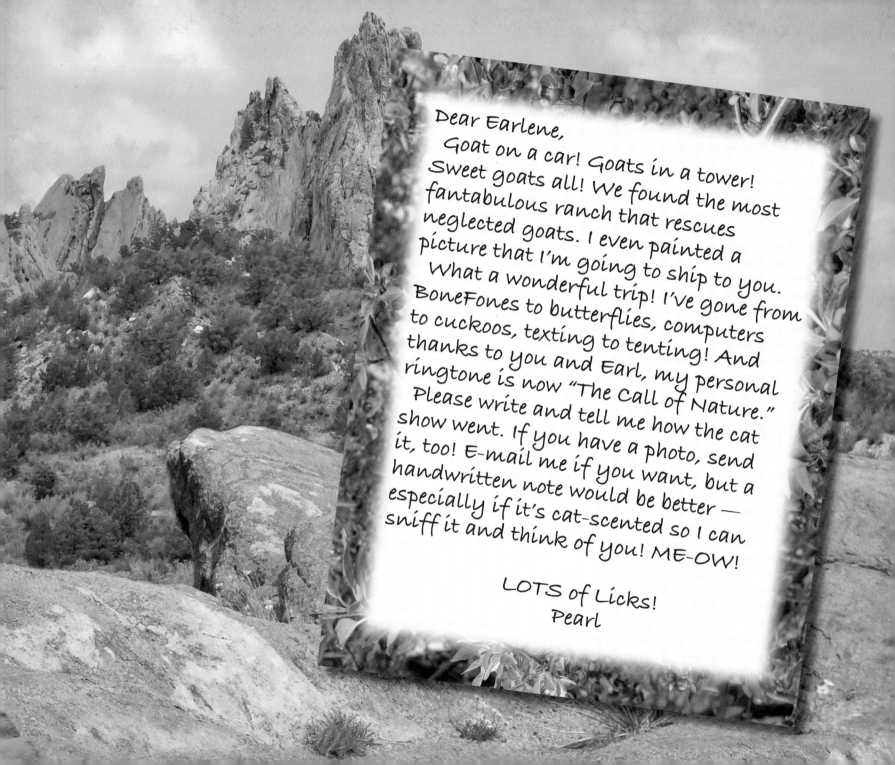

Dear Earlene,

Goat on a car! Goats in a tower! Sweet goats all! We found the most fantabulous ranch that rescues neglected goats. I even painted a picture that I'm going to ship to you. What a wonderful trip! I've gone from BoneFones to butterflies, computers to cuckoos, texting to tenting! And thanks to you and Earl, my personal ringtone is now "The Call of Nature." Please write and tell me how the cat show went. If you have a photo, send it, too! E-mail me if you want, but a handwritten note would be better — especially if it's cat-scented so I can sniff it and think of you! ME-OW!

LOTS of Licks!
Pearl

Our thanks to:

- Buster, who plays Earl and Earlene, and Barney, who plays Pearl, LOTS of Love! Cindy and Kirby.
- Editing assistance, Jennie Kaufman, Brooklyn, N.Y., and Paul Wood, Champaign, Ill.
- Cover: Wilborn Creek Beach, Lake Shelbyville, Ill.; dress by Hooey Batiks, Jill Miller, Urbana, Ill.
- Title page, wildflowers at Lake Shelbyville, Ill.
- Page 2, framed photograph, Bobo Pringle.
- Page 3, models, Charlene Anchor and her cat, Andy, Champaign, Ill.
- Page 4, Carl and Mary Bialeschki Farm, Tolono, Ill.; dress by Hooey Batiks, Jill Miller.
- Pages 6, 7 & 24, VW Beetle used with permission of Volkswagen of America Inc., Auburn Hills, Mich.
- Page 7, gas station, Mid America Motorworks, Effingham, Ill., owner Mike Yager; attendant model, Tessa Mae, owner Kirk Birch, Bement, Ill.; license plate model, Timber, owner Lois Olson, Pesotum, Ill.
- Page 8, Friends Cafe, Sidell, Ill., Sidell Historical Society; waitress model, Annie, owner Arnie Skillestad, Champaign, Ill., and Charlie, owner Jackie Worden, Charleston, Ill.
- Page 9, Ralphs Laundry, Elizabethtown, Ill., owners Charles and Eula Mae Ralph.
- Page 10, Wolf Creek State Park, Lake Shelbyville, Ill.
- Page 11, Homer Lake, Champaign County (Ill.) Forest Preserve District.
- Page 13, Rhoadside Custard, Mattoon, Ill., owners Ron and Laurie Rhoads.
- Page 14, Garden of the Gods, Shawnee National Forest, southern Illinois.
- Page 15, Walnut Point State Park, rural Oakland, Ill.
- Pages 16-17, Crystal Lake Park, Urbana, Ill., Urbana Park District; model Greg Kline, Champaign, Ill.
- Page 18, Hairpin Beauty Salon, Mahomet, Ill., owner Sara Heath; poster model, Tessa Mae; magazine poodle, Thistle, owner Margaret G. DeCardy, Champaign, Ill.
- Page 19, Craig's Barbershop, Jacksonville, Ill., owner John F. Green; barber model, Otto, owners Kevin and Kelly Pringle, Casey, Ill.
- Page 20, Blue Swallow Motel, Tucumcari, N.M., owners Bill Kinder and Terri Johnson.
- Page 21, Eagle Creek State Park, Lake Shelbyville, Ill.
- Page 22, Rural northeastern New Mexico.
- Page 23, Eagle Creek State Park, Lake Shelbyville, Ill.
- Page 24, State Route 104, near Conchas Lake State Park, N.M.
- Page 25, Illini Cat Club cat show, Savoy, Ill.
- Pages 26-27, Rural Cave-in-Rock, Ill.
- Page 28, Corvair, owners Terry and Nancy Kirk, Tuscola, Ill.; accordion courtesy of Charlene Anchor.
- Page 29, Goat tower, near Wolf Creek State Park, Ill., owners Dave and Marcia Johnson.
- Pages 30-31, Garden of the Gods, Colorado Springs, Colo.
- Page 32, White Sands National Monument, near Alamogordo, N. M.; Pearl's boots courtesy Rebecca Mabry, Homer, Ill.